This Little Tiger book
belongs to:

_____

_____

_____

Is It Christ

For Christmas Preparers everywhere.
Merry Christmas! Love, Jane xx — JC

LITTLE TIGER PRESS
1 The Coda Centre, 189 Munster Road, London SW6 6AW
www.littletiger.co.uk

First published in Great Britain 2013
This edition published 2014

Text and illustrations copyright © Jane Chapman 2013

Visit Jane Chapman at www.ChapmanandWarnes.com

Jane Chapman has asserted her right to
be identified as the author and illustrator of this work
under the Copyright, Designs and Patents Act, 1988

ISBN 978-1-84895-650-6 • LTP/1400/0934/0614
2 4 6 8 10 9 7 5 3

Jane Chapman

mas Yet?

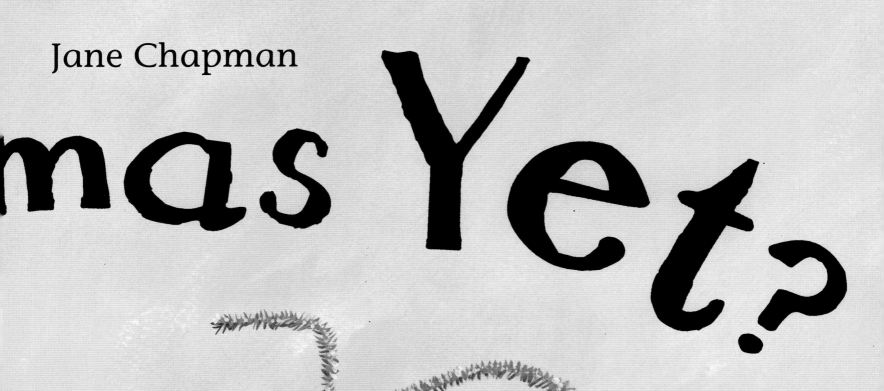

LITTLE TIGER PRESS
London

"FASTER, RUDOLPH, FASTER!"

yelled Ted, flying about with his toys, in his super Santa hat.

"Watch out, Santa!" Big Bear grinned.

"Your reindeer are out of control!"

"Christmas is coming! Hooray!" sang Ted.

He just COULD NOT WAIT.

"Big Bear!"

"Yes?"

"Is it Christmas yet?"

"Not yet."

"Big Bear!"

"Yes?"

"Is it Christmas yet?"

"Soon . . ."

"Big Bear!"
"**WHAT?**"
"Is it **SOON NOW?**"
"**NO**," growled Big Bear.
"We have to wrap all the
presents, bake the cake,
find the tree . . ."
"I'll help!" beamed Ted.
"I'm a good wrapper-upper."

zzzzzzzzzzpft!

But wrapping was tricky . . .
and surprisingly sticky!

"Is it Christmas yet?" mumbled
a tangle of ribbons and paper.

"Nearly," sighed Big Bear, "but we
still have to bake the cake . . ."

"Ready, Teddy, cook!"
laughed Ted with delight.

SPLODGE!

Whoosh!

PLOP!

Pip!

Big Bear popped the
cake in the oven.
   "Is it ready yet?"
sang Ted.

"NOT YET!" Big Bear
grumbled. "And it's not Christmas yet either."

"**WHEN** will it be Christmas?"
moaned Ted.
"**NOT YET!**" huffed Big Bear.
"We still need a Christmas tree . . ."

"I **LOVE** Christmas trees!"
grinned the little bear. "Come on!"

The woods were sparkling
with snow as two busy bears
searched for their tree.
But Ted was picky.

"TOO SMALL . . ."

"Ah, this one is **PERFECT!**"

"Really . . . ?" mumbled Big Bear.

Big Bear and Ted **HEAVED** …

and **HUFFED** …

and **PULLED**…

and **PUFFED**…

All the way home.

But the tree would not fit
through the front door . . .

or the back door . . .

And when they tried to pull it
through the window . . .

SNAP!

"I DON'T BELIEVE IT!"

moaned Big Bear.

Ted flumped down in a heap.

"OH NOOOOOOOOOOO!" he wailed.

Big Bear gave his little bear an enormous
Big Bear Hug. "We can fix this," he whispered
gently, "me and you. You're a great fixer-upper!"
"Oh **YES**!" whooped Ted.

Together, the bears taped up their tree.
Soon they were twirling tinsel and
scattering stars!

"Whoohoo! Bullseye!" cried
Big Bear, pinging the biggest
star to the top.

Ted yawned, "Is . . . it . . .
nearly . . . ?"

" . . .zzzZZZZZZZZZZ!"

"Yes, Teddy," whispered Big Bear, carrying him up to bed. "It's very, very nearly . . ."

More Christmas favourites from Little Tiger Press...

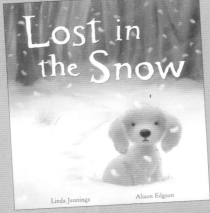

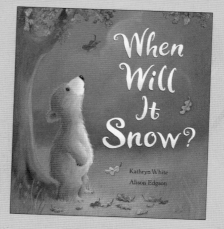
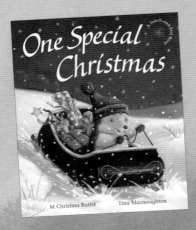

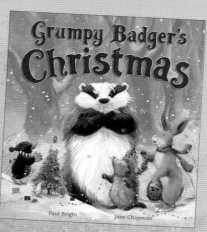